Albie

For Georgie
and in memory of Coo

First published in hardback in Great Britain by HarperCollins Publishers Ltd in 2002
First published in paperback by Collins Picture Books in 2002

1 3 5 7 9 10 8 6 4 2
ISBN: 978-0-00-783789-2

Collins Picture Books is an imprint of the Children's Division, part of HarperCollins Publishers Ltd.

Text copyright © Andy Cutbill/Ripping Gags Ltd 2002
Illustrations copyright Andy Cutbill/Ripping Gags Ltd and HarperCollins Publishers Ltd 2002

Based on the television series *Albie* © Cosgrove Hall Films Ltd

The HarperCollins website address is: www.fireandwater.com

Printed and bound in Malaysia

Albie

by

Andy Cutbill

ILLUSTRATIONS BY

Andy Cutbill and Mark Stacey

An imprint of HarperCollins*Publishers*

It was just another
ordinary day.

Albie was sitting in his

paddling pool when…

"Excuse me," asked a hippo, "can I borrow
a towel?"

Albie was stunned. "What are you doing in
my paddling pool?" he asked.

"*Your* paddling pool?" replied the hippo.
"This is *my* watering-hole!" And he picked up
the rubber pool and charged off.

"Wait!" shouted Albie. He ran off after
the hippo…

...straight into a tree.

"Oow!" shrieked Albie as a zebra holding a
TV set fell on top of him.

"What on earth do you think you're doing?"
asked the zebra.

"I'm sorry," said Albie," but I'm hunting for
a hippo."

"Well you won't find any hippos here," said
the zebra.

"Why not?" asked Albie.

"Because hippos can't climb trees!"

Meanwhile, back indoors, Albie's sister, Mary, was sitting down to watch her favourite television programme when…

"ALBIE!" yelled Mary. "Where's the TV?"

"Flips!" gasped Albie.

"Scarper!" yelled the zebra,
and he shot back up the tree.

Albie fled into the long grass.

"Do you mind?" cried a herd of buffaloes.

"It's polite to knock."

"I'm sorry," said Albie, panting. "My sister's after me. She thinks I've got the TV…"

Albie stopped. "That's our bath," he said. "From our bathroom!"

"Ah, yes," said one of the buffaloes. "We were borrowing it."

"But Mary will go mad!" spluttered Albie.

"ALBIE!"

came Mary's voice. "Is that you?"

"Oh, flips!" cried Albie.

"Run for your lives!"

Mary waded into the long grass.

"ALL

LLLLLLBBBiiiiiiiiiiii iiiiiiiii

eeeee!" yelled Mary.

But Albie was already heading

for the garage.

"Phew!" said Albie. "I'll be safe in here."

"Care for an anchovy cocktail?" came a voice.

"Ahhhh!" wailed Albie. "What are you doing in the freezer?"

"We thought we'd have a party," said a penguin. "Lovely weather for it, don't you think?"

"But you can't," panicked Albie. "My sister will go berserk."

"We'll invite her too," said another penguin.

"ALBIE!" shouted Mary, opening the door. "Where's the TV?" Then Mary saw the mess. "What on earth are you doing?" she gasped.

"It's not my fault," said Albie.

"Really?" said Mary.

"It's the penguins. In the freezer," said Albie. "But it was the zebras who…"

"Borrowed the TV?" sneered Mary.

"You've met them too?" asked Albie.

"I was kidding!" screamed Mary.

"It's not fair," said Albie. "The hippo started it.
He stole my paddling pool!"

"This paddling pool,
by any chance?"
screeched Mary.

"B…b…b…but…" said Albie.
"I've had enough, Albie.
I'm telling on you!"
said Mary.

And she stomped
towards the
kitchen door.

"I'm in real trouble now," Albie sighed.
"Silly paddling pool.
Stupid hippo."

"Me? Stupid?" said the hippo. "Well, you can keep your silly paddling pool. I'm making a much bigger watering-hole."

"Where?" asked Albie.
"Over there," said the
hippo. "I'm just waiting
for it to fill up."

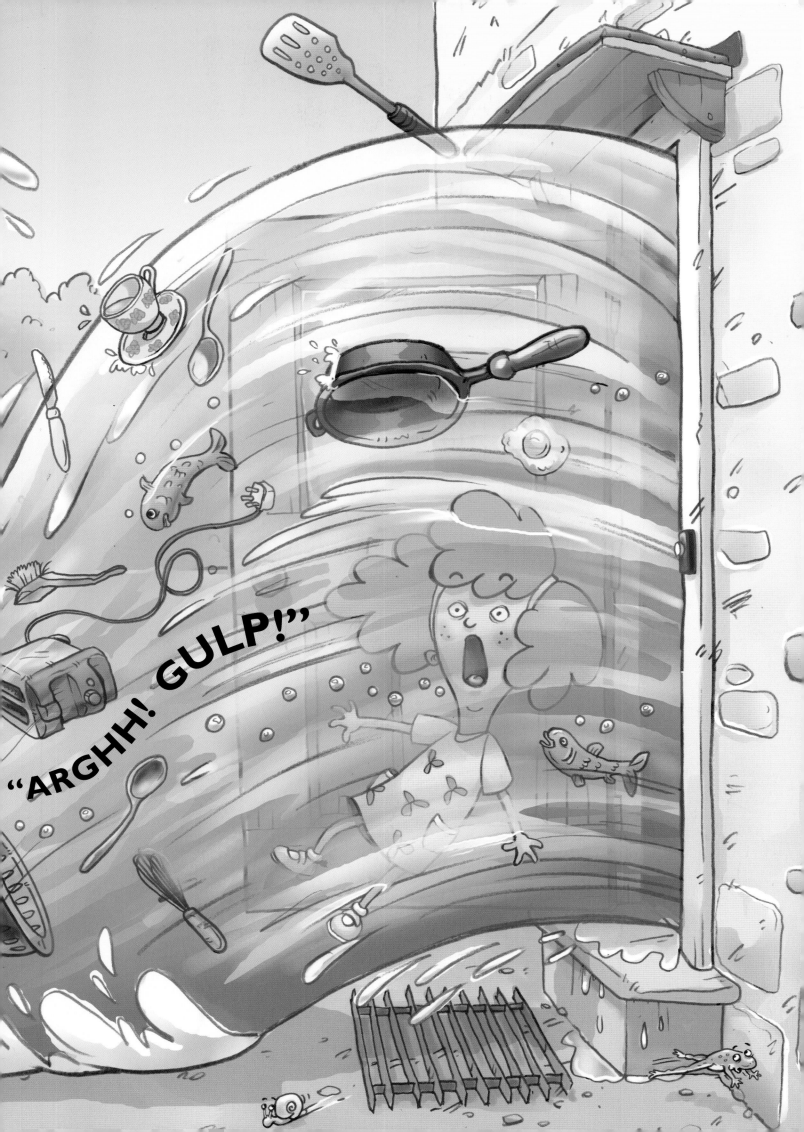

"AALLLLLBBBiiiiiieeeee!"

"Oh flips!" said Albie.